Hi and Lois in
CROQUET
FOR A DAY

by MORT WALKER and DIK BROWNE

TOR

A TOM DOHERTY ASSOCIATES BOOK
NEW YORK

HI AND LOIS: CROQUET FOR A DAY

Copyright © 1983, 1989 by King Features Syndicate

A TOR Book
Published by Tom Doherty Associates, Inc.
49 West 24 Street
New York, NY 10010

ISBN: 0-812-50311-2   Can. ISBN: 0-812-50312-0

First edition: October 1989

Printed in the United States of America

0 9 8 7 6 5 4 3 2 1

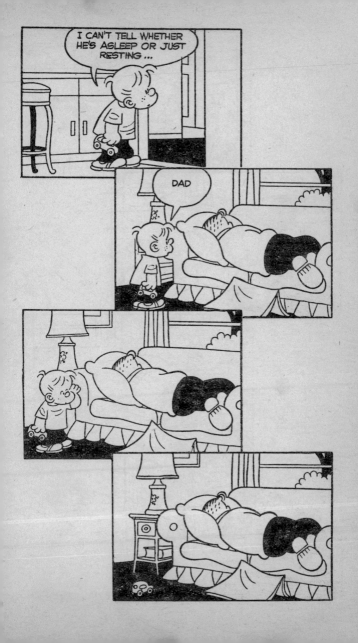

1-14

7-25

UH, LOIS, DID CHIP'S REPORT CARD COME TODAY?

NO, IT'S NOT DUE FOR TWO WEEKS

1-13

OH, OH, IT'S GOING TO BE A DOOZY!!

HAGAR THE HORRIBLE

☐ 56762-5   HAGAR THE HORRIBLE: VIKINGS ARE FUN $2.95
☐ 56763-2   Canada $3.95

☐ 56790-0   HAGAR THE HORRIBLE: OUT ON A LIMB $1.95
☐ 56791-9   Canada $2.50

☐ 56788-9   HAGAR THE HORRIBLE: PILLAGE IDIOT $1.95
☐ 56789-7   Canada $2.50

☐ 56746-3   HAGAR THE HORRIBLE: $2.50
☐ 56747-1   ROOM FOR ONE MORE   Canada $3.50

☐ 50072-5   HAGAR: GANGWAY $2.95
☐ 50073-3   Canada $3.95

☐ 50560-3   HAGAR AND THE GOLDEN MAIDEN $2.95
☐ 50561-1   Canada $3.95

Buy them at your local bookstore or use this handy coupon:
Clip and mail this page with your order.

Publishers Book and Audio Mailing Service
P.O. Box 120159, Staten Island, NY 10312-0004

Please send me the book(s) I have checked above. I am enclosing $_____
(please add $1.25 for the first book, and $.25 for each additional book to
cover postage and handling. Send check or money order only—no CODs.)

Name _____

Address _____

City _____ State/Zip _____

Please allow six weeks for delivery. Prices subject to change without notice.